Aaron Awoke

Aaron Awoke

An Alphabet Story
by Marilee Robin Burton

Harper & Row, Publishers

Aaron Awoke

Copyright © 1982 by Marilee Robin Burton

Library of Congress Cataloging in Publication Data
Burton, Marilee Robin.
   Aaron awoke.

   Summary: Aaron's actions follow the alphabet in a day on the farm.
   [1. Alphabet.   2. Farm life—Fiction]   I. Title.
PZ7.B9534Aar 1982   [E]   81-48638
ISBN 0-06-020891-0   AACR2
ISBN 0-06-020892-9 (lib. bdg.)

First Edition

2183639

for Sharon

Aaron awoke

Bathed in bubbles

Combed his curls

Dressed for the day

Entered the barn

Fed the chickens

Gathered the eggs

Hitched his horse

Invited friends for dinner

Jogged home

Kindled the fire

Ladled the lentils

Measured the mushrooms

Nibbled and noshed

Opened the door

Pulled out puzzles and paints

Quieted the dog

Rested on the rug

Sat down to supper

Told tall tales

Unfolded the guest beds

Visited quietly

Whispered, "Sweet dreams"

XXXed good night

Yawned

ZZZZZ